D0717415

Rosie & Jim
and the Snowman

By John Cunliffe Illustrated by Joan and Jane Hickson

A Ragdoll Production for Central Independent Television

Scholastic Children's Books,
Scholastic Publications Ltd,
7-9 Pratt Street, London NW1 0AE, UK

Scholastic Inc.,
555 Broadway, New York, NY10012-3999,
USA

Scholastic Canada Ltd,
123 Newkirk Road, Richmond Hill,
Ontario, Canada L4C 3G5

Ashton Scholastic Pty Ltd,
PO Box 579, Gosford, New South Wales,
Australia

Ashton Scholastic Ltd
Private Bag 92801, Penrose, Auckland,
New Zealand

First published by Scholastic Publications Ltd, 1993

Based on the Central Independent Television series
produced by Ragdoll Productions

ISBN 0 590 54103 X

Typeset by Rapid Reprographics
Printed in Hong Kong by the Paramount Printing Group

One very cold morning, Rosie said,
"Jim; there's a big light outside. Pop
your head out, noggin, and see
what it is."

Jim poked his head out.

"Rosie! Rosie! Come and see! It's
not a big light! It's...it's...all white...
sugar, Rosie. Sugar everywhere."

"Sugar?" said Rosie, coming to look. "Ooooh, who's done that?"

The boat, and the houses, and the trees, and the path by the canal, were all covered in white stuff, such as Rosie and Jim had never seen before.

"Lovely," said Rosie, "let's have a taste."

She scooped up a handful of the white stuff and put it in her mouth.

"Ooooohhh...errrrrrrr, noodle-noggin-fizzpot, it's *not* sugar, it's all wet...and cold...and fizzy!"

Jim had a taste.

"It's nice, Rosie. It's like ice-cream. Mmmmm, but, no, it isn't sugar. At least, not like the sugar John gets at the shop."

"It's made my hands all wet!" said Rosie.

"But, Rosie," said Jim, "where did it all come from?"

"How do I know, noggin? Let's listen. John might say something."

When John woke up, he *did* say

something! He shivered, and stoked
up the stove, and said,"Brrrrrr...here
comes winter! My goodness, there *is*
a lot of snow! But isn't it pretty?
Now, where did I put my camera?"

Rosie whispered to Jim. "Did you hear that, Jim?"

"Yes, Rosie. He called it *snow*."

"And, Jim, he wants to take a picture of it."

"He must like it."

John went outside to clear the snow off the boat. Rosie and Jim could hear the shouts of children playing in the snow.

John came in for his shopping-bag. Duck quacked, and Rosie said, "Ducky's quacking. We can go out, now, Jim. Get your bag, and we'll collect some of this snow. It sounds fun to play with."

Jim rushed out of the door, then
rushed back again, bumping hard
into Rosie.

"Ow! Noggin! Look where you're
going!" said Rosie.

"Oh, Rosie, there's a great monster
out there! A great big...a...a..."

"A what?" said Rosie. "What is it,
fizz-pot? Not another sheep?"

"No, it's not a sheep, Rosie. It's—it's a snow monster!"

"A snow monster? Oooh, there's no such thing. Let me see," said Rosie, and she ran up the steps.

15

Rosie jumped back into the cabin, and bumped hard into Jim, and they tumbled all in a heap on the floor. They sat up, and rubbed themselves, and looked at each other.

"What is it, Rosie?"

"What is it, Jim?"

"It might be... a snow monster."

"Perhaps," said Rosie, "perhaps it made all this snow."

"If we sit very quiet," said Jim."

"And don't make any noise," said Rosie.

"Then it'll go away."

"And not gobble us up."

Rosie and Jim sat still and quiet a long time.

Then, Jim said, "Rosie. Have a peep. See if it's gone."

Rosie peeped through a crack in the shutter. "It's still there."

"What's it doing?"

"Nothing."

"Nothing?"

"Just standing there," said Rosie.
   Rosie and Jim watched the
monster for a long time. It never
moved.
   "Let's go and look," said Jim.

"Slowly," said Rosie, "and quietly."

Two very slow and very quiet ragdolls crept out of the boat. The monster stood and looked at them. It did not move. It made no sound. They crept closer. Closer.

"It's white," said Jim.

"Like the snow," said Rosie.

"Do you think..." said Jim. "Rosie, do you think...?"

But Jim never finished what he wanted to say. Some children came running along the tow-path. They were jumping, and rolling, and sliding, and snowballing, and playing in the snow.

When they saw Rosie and Jim and the monster, a girl shouted, "Look! A snowman!"

"And Rosie and Jim!" shouted the others. "Come on!"

"A *snowman*?" said Rosie. "Did you hear that, Jim? They called the monster a *snowman*. That's what it is."

"And they're coming to play with it," said Jim.

"And us," said Rosie.

Rosie and Jim played in the snow with the children. What a time they all had! The children showed Rosie and Jim how to make a snowman. They made a snow-Rosie and a snow-Jim. They made a snowdog and a snowcat. They even made a snowduck, and a snow-John.

Tea-time came all too soon. Far
away, the children's mothers called
them in.

"We'll have to go," they said.

"Time for tea."

"And bed."

"Come again," said Rosie.

"Tomorrow," said Jim.

"Sure," said the children. "We'll be
back. Bye!"

They ran off, through the snow.
Duck quacked.

"Time for us," said Rosie.

"We've played too long," said
Jim. Rosie and Jim jumped into the
boat, just in time to hide from John,
as he came slowly along the path,
loaded up with his shopping.

"Never mind," said Rosie, "we still
have some snow to play with. I
filled my bag with it."

When she looked, her bag was all wet and soggy, and the snow had gone.

"Ooooh, noggin," she said, "where has it gone?"

John had a surprise, when he saw
all the snow-creatures.

Jim woke up in the night, and said,
"We still don't know where it came
from."

"What, noggin?" said Rosie,
sleepily.

"The snow."

"Go to sleep," said Rosie, "and never mind where it comes from."

The next morning, they woke up, and saw snow falling out of the sky.

"There you are," said Rosie.

"What?" said Jim.

"That's where it comes from. The sky."

"But who makes it?" said Jim.

"Ooooh, noggin," said Rosie. "Where do your questions come from?"

"They just come," said Jim.

"Like the snow," said Rosie.

"Let's go and play," said Jim. So they did.